THE
GOOD
REVEREND

Thou shalt not kill.

E. DEAN ARNOLD

THE
GOOD
REVEREND

Thou shalt not kill.

PENDIUM
PUBLISHING HOUSE
514-201 DANIELS STREET
RALEIGH, NC 27605

For information, please visit our Web site at
www.pendiumpublishing.com

PENDIUM Publishing and its logo
are registered trademarks.

The Good Reverend
by E. Dean Arnold

Copyright © E. Dean Arnold, 2020
All Rights Reserved.

ISBN: 978-1-944348-85-4

PUBLISHER'S NOTE:

Without limiting the rights under the copyright reserved above, no part of this publication may be reproduced, stored in or introduced into a retrieval system, or transmitted, in any form, or by any means (electronic, mechanical, photocopying, recording, or otherwise), without the prior written permission of both the copyright owner and the above publisher of this book.

If you purchased this book without a cover you should be aware that the book is stolen property. It was reported as "unsold and destroyed" to the publisher and neither the author nor the publisher has received any payment for this "stripped book."

This book is printed on acid-free paper.

Dedicated to my friends and family – who've shown me nothing but support.

ALSO BY
E. DEAN ARNOLD

MR. JONES

a story by

EDWARD DEAN ARNOLD

Available at Amazon.com

CONTENTS

Also by E. Dean Arnold vii

Chapter One 1

Chapter Two 20

Chapter Three 38

Chapter Four 53

Chapter Five 65

Foul (Coming Soon) 85

CHAPTER ONE

Shonda knew, if she could just get Juror #3 to pick up her pencil, then this would be a sure win.

It was the day of final arguments in the case of Becky Sarnoff, a woman accused of a hit and run. Miss Sarnoff had been leaving her job as a waitress in a diner around the same time that another car – matching the make, color, and model of hers, granted – had driven a swath of destruction through the local mall's parking lot. It crashed through signs, dented a long line of cars, and tore up grassy medians. Shonda had let out a long whistle when she saw the full price tag for the incident, but she took the case after one interview of Miss Sarnoff. Becky was an admitted alcoholic, but with a chip that promised she hadn't touched a drop in over a decade. It didn't help that her car was an old jalopy that looked like it had been driven through a half dozen shopping malls on its own, but Shonda could tell she was innocent. So could her team, and they all found that a heartwarming and refreshing change.

It was one that affected wardrobe too. If you worked for Shonda long enough, you learned to tell what she thought of her client by what she wore on her feet to work. When she was worried that she was defending a guilty party – like with that tax evasion creep last month – Shonda always wore a black pair of platforms that made not a hint of noise as she moved back and forth across the buffed tile of the courtroom floor. It was a telltale sign that she was on her back foot, in a way. She didn't want to overstep her presence when she knew she was trying to get away with something (which, with the tax evasion creep, she certainly had).

Today, however, she was in her red heels.

When Shonda was at max confidence – especially when that confidence was to the betterment of a client *who was innocent* – she always wore the same set of crimson dynamos that gave her footfalls a fierce staccato rhythm that sounded like a call to arms as she cross examined. She loved that sound – when her steps were sure – and she let them propel her into her final argument. Facing her jury, and she was really feeling like they were hers, she began with a bit of a ruse that wasn't going to feel like a home run at first. That was okay, she wasn't afraid to bide her time and build to sway opinion at speech's end. She cocked her head and gave a bit of a shrug. "We've all done wrong… isn't that right?"

The jury looked to each other, not sure what to say… and a bit surprised that Shonda was opening with such a weak presumption. She went on, however, building to her point like a potter working clay. "The bulk of the prosecution's case hasn't relied on evidence. It hasn't really needed to, has it? No. Instead, they've built an entire argument that depends on whether my client is telling the truth." She took one tiny step toward the jury. Then a second – but not a third. No, two was just right. Two was 'leaning in' like they were confidantes. Three would have been presumptuous. She lifted a hand to her mouth, whispering to the jury like they were a pack of drinking buddies, "Well, we're all liars, right? That's the only real truth, isn't it?"

There was one fleeting moment here where her opponent – a balding but capable little cuss of a lawyer named Wallace Sturbridge – thought Shonda had made a mistake, and she took a bit of delight in that: *That's okay, Wally. It's good to want things.* He was right that she was skating right up to the edge, sympathizing with liars. Both Wally and Shonda watched Juror #3 closely as her eyes narrowed at the sacrilege. Juror #3, you see, *didn't* consider herself a liar. Shonda knew that. This was all just her set up. She could tell Juror #3 considered herself a "good," honest woman. She had excellent posture, never gave the slightest snicker at inappropriate jokes, and wore a tiny cross over her turtleneck that absolutely, positively kept her from ever showing the slightest bit of cleavage or curvature of the breast – the woman reminded Shonda a great deal of her mother, actually. Her mother walks the walk. Shonda knew women like Juror #3 deeply – which meant she knew how to change their minds too.

Juror #3 was the only one who hadn't been taking notes during the entire trial. Every one of the jurors had been furnished with the same drab, court-issued pad and pencil. Shonda knew those pads well. Most juries are split down the middle between two different types of people, the "scribblers" and the "Tolstoys" – those who doodled and those who feverishly wrote down far too many notes. Shonda was amazed at how much some people wrote down – didn't they realize that, if they needed to write it all down, Shonda wasn't doing her job. Her defenses were a kind of performance art. If they would just sit back and let her dazzle them with her show, it would be as easy as pie to keep up with the facts. Hammering the pertinent facts was her job. No matter which group each juror belonged to, however, they all gave off a thousand signs in the way they jotted down on their pads as to how they were feeling about the case. Shonda knew what it meant when a scribbler paused to listen to a detail, or when a Tolstoy started writing faster and more feverishly. She knew just how to cater her performance to an audience of either style.

Ultimately, however, the final decisions of many juries – including this one – rested on the will of one person from a mysterious third category. Juror #3 was a *listener*. She hadn't even touched her pad. It was like she didn't know what it was for or, more accurately, like she didn't need it at all. Some would see that as Juror #3 being lazy, detached… but Shonda knew – and she suspected that Wally did too – that Juror #3 had already made her mind up. Juror #3 didn't trust Shonda's client. This was probably due to the fact that, unlike her, Becky showed *plenty* of cleavage. This was probably due to the sad reality that it increased her tips. Becky lived on those tips and Juror #3 probably hadn't lost sweat on a rent check her entire life.

This wasn't the time to judge either woman over the other, however. It was time for Shonda to play the game and, in this risky moment, Juror #3 wasn't going to be taking much of a liking to Shonda either. When Shonda had said, "We're all liars, right?," the rest of the jury had collectively nodded, conceded, agreed…

… but not #3. No. Juror #3 considered her record clean, her honesty spotless. It wasn't Shonda's job to challenge that, but to appeal to it. So she followed that set up question straight into Juror #3's eyes and challenged it herself. "*No*. Not all of us, right? Some of us pride ourselves on our honesty." This got a small, almost-imperceptible nod from Juror #3. Almost nothing, but Shonda knew it meant it was time to seal the deal. "Those of us that aren't liars know what it is to be falsely accused, to fight back, provide full transparency. Look at the prosecution's case, witnesses unavailable, moments they can't remember, working hard to hold to their 'truth.' Not my client. She remembers everything, even when it doesn't help her case. No waffling. No lost records. You can tell which of us are honest because our lives are open books. We live by what the Bible says. My client lets her yes be yes and her no… no." *That* was how Shonda got Juror #3. Scripture. She quoted the book of Matthew and it had shot right into the core of Juror #3 like a lightning bolt.

Juror #3 picked up her pencil.

Shonda smiled.

After her client was found not guilty, Shonda gave a victory tour around the courthouse steps. She was delighted to meet the rest of Becky's family, who had come from all around to offer support and fill the courtroom behind her. "You all being here had a lot to do with it. Thank you." The family didn't want to hear a thing about any of that. They showered Shonda with hugs and gifts, including a homemade pencil cup decorated by Becky's young daughter, Jessica. "I'll cherish this. Thank you."

The little girl smirked and said, "My mommy says your desk is a mess." They all laughed at the honesty.

"Well, it'll be a lot less messy now because of you."

Shonda tussled the little girl's hair and gave a long hug to Becky, whose eyes were tearing with relief. The trial had been hard on her. She didn't have anywhere near the money to cover the damages – or Shonda's fee – had they lost. When she explained that to Shonda at their first meeting, however, she had simply reassured her, "Well, in that case, let's just not lose. How about that for a battle plan?"

Becky stammered for words to show appreciation, to which Shonda just replied, "You can thank me by hiring me to conduct your countersuit. That mall fumbled with its security camera game and you and Jessica went through great hardship because of it. It's time for celebration now, but after let's get to work on winning you a little bit of a settlement to take your daughter to Disneyland." That made Jessica's eyes light up and Shonda winked as her heels clicked away.

Next up was a dull line of handshakes from other lawyers and suits that wanted to congratulate her on a well-handled case. Wally gave a bow of defeat, "I thought I had you there at the end, just for a moment."

She gave him a friendly – but somewhat emasculating – touch on the shoulder. "Isn't that sweet. Wally thought he was gonna come out on top." She shared a sly smile with Wally. They were often rivals, but the truth was also that he genuinely respected her. When they had first met, she was just a nobody lawyer wannabe, not even an up-and-comer yet. Her beauty was both an asset and a detriment in that era of her career. The boy's club didn't take her seriously and, more often than she liked to think about, they would make passes at her behind closed doors.

There had been an unfortunate shady period where Shonda knew she was baring an unjust and mistaken scarlet letter of sorts. It was the worst kept secret in town that many members of the male-dominated Atlanta lawyer scene whispered about who she must have slept with to get where she had gotten in so short a time. There was no truer proof of the entrenched sexism in her profession or the region itself than the sheer disbelief some men carried at the idea of a woman daring to outshine them at every turn. She was proud to know that she had never crossed that line, and didn't mind making sure she looked good doing it to twist the knife in her critics' backs all the more.

Wally, on the other hand, was a member of another class of man. He was a gentleman. After a few cases against each other, the poor guy had given a knock on her office door and gave her a very timid and nervous ask out to dinner. Shonda had been relieved to have the old stand-by of "Wally, we really shouldn't. It would cross a professional line." The truth was, the little guy was a bit of a dweeb. They both knew he was hitting a little above his weight on asking her out. She was a head-turner and he looked like, well, a lawyer. Still, in a world of men counting her out, getting away with inappropriate remarks, or even placing a hand where they knew it didn't belong, it was a breath of fresh air to actually know a man who was old-fashioned enough to not be a monster. She had never made fun of him behind his back about it, and was genuinely happy for him when he got married a couple of years later. They had a lot of water under the bridge, but she was genuinely happy whenever she learned he was going up against her. They fought fair against each other always. That was starting to sadly be a limited quality these days.

Her next handshake was with a man who was the exact opposite of Wally. Jackson Moreland was one of the hottest attorneys in the region. He wore a suit better than any man his age had any business to, and he sported the strongest jawline that she had ever known. All the assurance of a veteran lawyer with decades more experience, all packed into an achingly attractive young body. They had shared a lunch once at a restaurant near the courthouse, and Shonda still remembered thinking about letting her calf kick out, just a bit, to brush up against his leg. *That* feeling, that girlish exhilaration at the idea of even a casual "accidental" touch, had been the closest she had ever come to crossing the line.

She often wondered what she would have done if he had made a move on her that afternoon. The truth was, however, that he definitely did not. He kept things intimate and whispered, but professional, and Shonda had a feeling he knew that must drive some women crazy. Moreland had the nerve to be not only one of the best lawyers in town – he was certainly the most attractive – and here he was having the nerve to never hit on her.

He did want her in another way, however. He, like many of the partnered lawyers in the city, wanted her to join his firm. There were many entities courting her these days – enough that she was just starting to come to terms with the fact that she was kind of a big deal. Wally had mentioned this to her earlier in the week, listing off the top firms that she was rumored to be closely courting. She had enjoyed letting him know that he didn't even know about the best three. Moreland was with one of those: Kaplan & Warren & Statham & Beauregard. It was no secret that Jackson was ravenous to add a "& Moreland" to that already too-much-of-a-mouthful company name. Bringing aboard an up-and-coming successful attorney at the top of her game – say, a Shonda Lassiter for example – would certainly be a help on his way to putting his name on their dull but impressive business cards and large metal nameplate that dominated the front lobby.

That, however, wasn't Shonda's dream at all. No, there was no desire in her to be one of the names on a list that made her firm's title too long for an average business card. She wasn't even intrigued by a corner office in a tall building. Shonda liked making her own coffee and having an office on the second floor, overlooking the street just right. She liked being down near the people – the actual people – who she was working for. She also preferred those people to not be rich snobs. Jackson Moreland's life was lousy with rich snobs. He magically wasn't becoming one himself, but he knew just what watch to wear and where to take the snobs for dinner, cigars, or pole dancing so that he could seal the deal. Shonda wanted clients that needed true help, not for a tax write-off to go away. As it was, she was so very close to fully achieving her dream – however it didn't look like it to many of the other lawyers in town…

… Shonda was on the verge of making partner in just five years at Kerns & Dunaway, one of the most highly regarded law firms in Atlanta (and one with a still not-bonkers-long name as well, so bonus, yeah?). Terrance Dunaway was the first person who ever assigned her a case. No professional lawyer ever put stake in her ability to succeed before him. He was a heartfelt mentor and friend and, no, he had *never* so much as let a dirty joke fly around her or anyone she knew. She had once overheard a rat-faced intern make a joke about her and Terrance and she almost put the kid through a wall. Only after the fact did she realize that, unlike any other jokes that had ever sent her over the edge, it wasn't the slight on her that pissed her off. It was the idea that they were disrespecting Terrance. He was the patron saint of her career in law.

It was only because of the shot he had given her that Shonda had become what she was now: a gladiator in Louboutins, with a tough exterior and confrontational nature that made her the "go-to" defender for high profile cases. She had a who's who roster of star clients, but her dreams involved bigger moves than just other law firms. The pieces were falling into place for her to leave her group practice and start her own law firm. She knew it would mean driving a worse car than Jackson – or

The Good Reverend

even Wally – but Shonda wanted fewer celebrity cases and more grassroots changing people's lives for the better. Terrance understood this. Many were worried that he was going to be mad when it finally came time for her to set off on her own. Shonda knew he understood her though. For anyone who truly knew Shonda, they knew she believed that the law was there to save people's lives; not just their tax returns or business dealings. She worked hardest when it was to save a family's rent check, to get back a grandmother's heirloom, or to keep a child's parent out of unfair jail time. She knew she only had to establish herself at Kerns & Dunaway for a few more months to establish herself well enough to create her own practice and failure was not an option – but she also knew that, no matter how she tried, not everything worked out the way she planned...

Breaking her from her glad-handing with the masses surrounding the courtroom doors, she suddenly felt a strong hand press to her arm. A voice, soft but deep, whispered into her ear: "Shonda, I need to speak to you. It's urgent."

At first, she bristled at whoever was taking her arm in such a way. She turned, about to protest and pull away, until she saw who it was. "Brice? What are you doing here?" Brice Larson was a good man, a former cop who had turned in his badge when he found corruption in his higher-ups. Because of his past, it was odd to see him in this part of the city, which was dominated by the courthouse and police department. Back when he was muscled off the force, Shonda had wondered if Brice was being too naïve about his career in law enforcement – what police department wasn't wracked with bribes and double-dealing? It had impressed her to watch as Brice stuck to his guns, but she was saddened to see later that it didn't exactly assure him a heroic exit or a very comfortable future. Instead, he had ended up working as Head of Security on what must have been the most boring beat in the greater Atlanta area...

Mountaintop was the largest mega-Church in the state and it was aiming to someday say the same about the nation. It broadcast every sermon internationally to the faithful, and wallpapered every highway on the East Coast with billboards proclaiming the words of the Christian Bible and the works of Jesus Christ. Four United States Presidents had attended services there over the decades (two of which the Church wasn't ashamed of). If you asked any homeless person in the city what building mattered to them most, it was Mountaintop Church. It was a monolith of social impact for Atlanta, a haven for lost souls everywhere, and its pastor just happened to be Shonda's stepfather.

Though Shonda had a checkered past with her powerful and outspoken stepdad, Brice had always been a staunch defender of his character. That faith of his, however, was being rocked today. "Shonda... it's Reverend Richards – your father. He's in trouble."

Shonda could tell by his eyes that that trouble just happened to be big. Without a word, she led him out of the courthouse and they hurried out into the parking lot toward Brice's car. "*What kind* of trouble?" she asked en route.

It felt like only moments later when Shonda found herself sitting across a police station interrogation table from Reverend Sherman Richards. She remembered that Brice drove her over here, but her brain was churning for the entire ride – chewing over the impossibility that he had whispered to her in the parking garage of the courthouse just before getting into his car: "Shonda… they think the Reverend killed a man."

That sentence was echoing in her mind and making her question if she was awake at all. *Crap. Has this all been a dream? Am I about to wake up and have to shower and get to the courthouse to defend Becky again?* The reality of the situation shook into clear focus, however, as Pastor Richards was led into the room before her. This was a man she was used to seeing in a crisp suit and tie behind a pulpit, his sermon being projected onto massive screens on the walls to either side. Here he was today, face awash in fear, and being roughly cuffed to a harsh metal table. Knowing it wasn't going to do any good, she attempted a protest on his behalf. "Officer, I know this man and, believe me, the handcuffs aren't necessar—"

Like she predicted, they weren't listening to her at all. Though he was a celebrity of the church circuit, this jailer didn't know the difference between Reverend Richards and any other car thief, drug dealer, or wife beater he was used to escorting down the halls of this place. He affixed one handcuff to Reverend Richards and the other to a stark metal ring on the table in the center of the room.

Shonda sat on the opposite side from him, having no idea what to say to the poor man, who was obviously beside himself with worry and fear. He was the one that broke the silence. Though he spoke in a stammer, you could tell he meant his words in an urgent and desperate way. It was a plea: "I didn't do it, Shonda."

Shonda had stared into a thousand faces as they told her that they "didn't do" something. It had been an agonizing thing to perfect, but she was now fully able to tell if someone saying such a thing was a lie or not – usually by the time the person had finished the sentence. Her heart still ached from the half a dozen cases in which she had been wrong about in the past, mostly at the start of her career when she was still green. Nowadays, however, she considered herself a human lie detector. She remembered, bringing a sour taste in her mouth, the last time she was wrong about it – a three-time murderer from Greensboro – and she shuddered at the thought. It gave her some comfort, in contrast, to count the years between that last failed diagnosis and now. She hasn't been wrong about guilt in over nine years. Reverend Richards, right there in front of her, wasn't lying. He hadn't done it. Shonda had known that, however, before he had even said it. Sometimes she didn't need to hear it from the mouth of the accused. Sometimes she could tell by the premise of the crime that it just didn't add up. Didn't seem right. Not one bit of any of this right here seemed right in the slightest.

The grisly information that was presented for her over the next hour shook her to the core. Her stepfather was being held under suspicion of first degree murder, and it was a murder most gruesome. A man had been found, strangled and stabbed, with his mouth stuffed with journal papers soaked in blood. Detectives were still piecing together what the papers said – and forensics was carefully probing deeper inside the victim's throat to see if more pages had been lodged further inside. However, the overwhelming evidence was becoming all too clear on the gore-stained pages. In careful script that was a calling card of the author, they discovered it was a letter from Reverend Richards himself. They were trying to make out more of the message that was delivered in such a grisly way but, for now, the only words that were discernible through the dead man's blood was the very last line, "I know what you did and this is how I want to forgive you." The damning message was even signed at the bottom. So few words, but they were all it took. It practically read like a confession of the crime.

Her brain was a whirl just trying to accept the circumstances of the day. She and her stepfather didn't see eye to eye on a lot of things, it was true – they had fought over law, religion, who sits where at Thanksgiving, how best to care for her mother – but she never considered him even capable of committing a crime, let alone first degree murder. Normally she called him Reverend Richards, as did most of the people in his life. Across this table, however, she was surprised as she called him: "Dad… what did you mean, 'I know what you did' – before we keep talking. I need to know the answer to that."

The question made his eyes well with emotion. He obviously knew the answer, and it terrified him to say it aloud. He shook his head and fell silent. After waiting long enough, Shonda stood. "I'm praying you didn't murder that man. But you *did* write that letter. When you're ready to talk about it, I'm ready to defend you." As she stepped out, she noticed those same high heel footfalls of hers. They sounded so confident back in her winning courtroom that morning. Now they sounded like they were echoing in a dark world of doubt.

Outside the room, Brice was surprised to see how much Shonda kept her composure. She was all business, giving the police a list of demands as to the pastor's treatment. "My client is not to share a cell with anybody. I want him under constant–"

An officer took an ill-advised route, interrupting her with a challenge. "Your client? Is that an official status? That's news to us."

Shonda knew they were right – her stepdad *hadn't* hired her… and she hadn't fully offered her services yet, either – but that didn't stop her from cutting violently through any red tape they were considering throwing up to get in the way. "Well, then here's news. I'm his lawyer. That's as official as you need to know. And when I represent one of your inmates, you know what that means. Keep him safe. Treat him legally. Or I will rain hell." The officer stayed quiet behind the desk, but Shonda didn't let him off the hook. "So we're good, right. We're clear?" Brice stifled a smirk as the officer only managed a slight nod in reply. He was clear. Shonda got no further argument throughout the precinct – a force to be reckoned with – as she strutted out of the station on a warpath.

Brice watched her keep that confident strut all the way out the door and across the sun-drenched parking lot on the way to his car. It was the kind of painfully humid day that could sap the energy out of just about anybody, yet she moved like an electrified gazelle. He had always been enamored of Shonda – hell, most of the men he knew were – but she had also always heavily intimidated him. His security work at her stepdad's church often sat them beside each other at dinners and functions. They were friendly, but he had always chosen to let his crush take the backseat to a healthy amount of respect… and a bit of fear. Over the years, that strategy had proven itself a winner. He knew quite a few guys who had suffered a tongue lashing when they tried to get too close. He considered her unattainable romantically, so he had grown to accept just being close acquaintances via family. Watching her power strut, however, was a sight to behold – even under such horrible circumstances as the conviction of a man who was such a father figure to him.

Once they reached Brice's car, however, he was suddenly privy to a side of Shonda that he didn't even know was possible. She slid into his passenger seat and didn't seem to hear him as he asked, "So, where are we headed?" He let the uncomfortable and charged silence hang there a moment, as her eyes seemed to lose themselves in the plastic pattern on the dashboard in front of her. She reached out an arm – Brice noticed it was shaking – and placed her hand flat on the dashboard. This seemed to steady her for a moment...

... then Shonda's shoulders started to pulse and quiver in a way that was easy for Brice to identify. She was obviously holding back a full-on tearful breakdown. He cast aside any cares about keeping a polite distance now, seeing only a person in need right there before him. He placed a hand on her arm. "It's okay. I feel the same way. Let it out."

She tried to brush this off, but her chest was beginning to heave. "I'm fine. I'm fine. Just drive. I don't want them to see."

Brice did as she desired. He rolled them out of the parking lot, far from any lawyers or police that she needed to shield her emotions from. As soon as they got around the corner, Shonda broke down into a fit of uncontrollable sobs. Brice drove on, occasionally letting out a small chirp of support that he couldn't tell if she was even hearing or not. "I understand. We all do. It's a lot to try and digest." Shonda just traced the back of her fingers down the window glass beside her and stared out as she wept, perfect makeup now running down her cheeks.

Heading away from the city center, Brice circled Centennial Olympic Park a few times, then meandered near the Botanical Gardens. His mind drifted to how the cruise of the city with her would make for a lovely afternoon under any other circumstances. Eventually, however, he felt it was time to try and help her focus and get back to the matter at hand. When he broke the silence and again asked her where she would like him to take her – assuring her that he was up to the task, no matter what action she thought was right – Shonda fumbled into her purse for a pair of sunglasses and slipped them on as she spoke. She seemed haunted by the answer even as it left her mouth. "I– I need to go see my mother."

CHAPTER TWO

Brice's humble car jarred with its surroundings as it pulled slowly to the front gate of the very un-humble home of Pastor Sherman and her mother. They were both used to the opulent McMansion that had been built a few years ago as a result of Mountaintop Church's massive expansion. Both of them also, however, had their own opinions on it. Even while the man was locked up across town, Shonda wasn't shy with hers. "Blessed are the poor, amiright?"

This won a smirk from Brice as he cruised them up the long driveway under the hot mid-day sun, but he was also quick to defend his mentor. "You should have seen the place the last Pastor lived in… but, as you know, it turned out he kind of deserved it."

Mountaintop's last pastor was caught skimming some "extra payroll" from the offering plates. It was an especially grievous finding, due to the fact that this was back when there wasn't much to skim from the Mountaintop community in the first place. The news had come right after the church council had cancelled both a getaway weekend for the Women's Group and a trip to a festival for the bell choir. To then find out that the very man who preached strict morality from the pulpit was also the biggest thief in the room almost ended the church forever. They instantly became the biggest gossip point in the greater Atlanta area and a shameful example for the Christian Church at large. National news outlets even had their fun, and the congregation was forced to watch their tragedy made fun by late night comedians. No one that went to the church lifted a finger to fight back against the criticisms because, well, all of the critiques were one hundred percent correct. They were used to braving the slings and arrows the secular world unleashed on the church whenever they could. That time, unfortunately, the target on their backs was sadly deserved.

It was Shonda's stepfather who had turned Mountaintop around. After the scandal, no pastor in the country wanted to even give a second thought to stepping up to face the challenge of healing the shattered mega-church. Pastor Sherman had been a wide-eyed young preacher at the time, with a diploma in religious studies in one hand and an empty resume in the other. He had shown up to his interview by the church council in a beat up station wagon that broke down in the parking lot. Somehow, he had used that weakness as a strength – holding up his hands with true humility and insisting that it was a sign from God that he had finally reached the place where he was destined to serve His will. "After all, if you don't hire me? I'm not sure how I'm even driving out of here." That story had then spread like wildfire, turning the public's opinion around in a way that then led to Mountaintop becoming an even <u>greater</u> force of good in the Atlanta area.

Brice had been there for all of that. His heart had been broken by the scandal surrounding the previous pastor. His faith in society had been shaken when he found corruption in the police system but then, when he was confronted with it in the Church? That almost ended him right then and there. He considered the months that followed to be the darkest of his life. Then his spirit had been fully renewed by the arrival of Pastor Sherman. It was the understatement of the century to say that he was a fan. "In my humble opinion, Pastor Sherman deserves an extra garage or two." Shonda thumbed to the mammoth side building attached to the main house. "Or three? Four? Your opinion's about the only 'humble' thing within a hundred acres right about now."

With a laugh, Brice brought the car to a stop. "Yeah, sorry. I do lose count of how many garages they put in. Still, he's a good man, Shonda. The best I've ever known." She nodded, knowing he was being sincere… but also knowing that the next few days were going to put that esteem to the ultimate test.

No matter how many garages her stepfather had, they were all open and full now, and the driveway was lined with other cars and Mountaintop shuttles as well. Even as they stepped across the gravel in the muggy Georgia sun, she could hear inside that they had arrived to a house in uproar. Of course they had – nothing about this was going to be anything but drama. As she approached the front door with dread, Shonda's eyes drank in the gigantic building that was far from the childhood home she remembered. As a little girl, Shonda had been raised in a perfectly humble little brick townhouse closer in to the city. Just suburban enough to be safe, just urban enough to still be vibrant.

The Good Reverend

She drove by that house every once in a while, remembering long lost days before they had lost her father in a car accident. Her memories were all family BBQs and outdoor exploration, holiday parties and the biggest fights being over the remote. She remembered her father as a good man, despite the fact that he seemed to have always been beleaguered by money. They hadn't been poor, but, even as a child, she knew her parents sweat over every check, burning midnight oil for her dance classes and worrying about how she was going to afford college. Those worried looks on her parents' faces had fueled her, however, especially after her mother was alone. She had ended up going to the best college that offered her a free ride. One of the most beautiful sights she ever saw was the relief that washed over her mother's face when she realized that her daughter was actually going to get to go to school. Her mother was many amazing things, but a self-made woman she was not. She had always been a kept woman – by good men, yes (and that was no small thing to be thankful for) – but a rather silent and doting wife all her life. Shonda had learned by watching her – she wasn't ever going to be anything like that. She was proud to be a part of showing her how women could make their own way in this world, and how beautiful it was when they did.

This mansion that she was so trepidatious about entering, however, was perhaps the biggest monument to her mother's subservience. It wasn't a home, but more of an immaculate estate that her mother, Grace, had earned the right to when she married the most respected pastor in the region. It was more of an edifice than a house, a monument to the success of the Mountaintop Church, whose stern board of directors had subsidized the home's creation in their annual budget. It had been designed by the Pastor from bottom to top – every shingle and tile chosen after too many debates over style. Shonda could remember having to take an Uber home when she drank too much on a visit, just to try and drown out their endless chatter over which wallpaper to put in the East Wing Bathroom (they went with Battleship Grey). Shonda was happy that her mother was so stable, but it sometimes sickened her to see her in this staid and perfectly-manicured suburban version of Downton Abbey.

At first, her mother had hilariously struggled to clean it all herself. Shonda had laughed and laughed when she came over to visit, only to find her mother throwing away what must have been her fortieth sponge just trying to clean the kitchen's immense battery of cabinets. It wasn't funny, conversely, when she caught her mom on a high ladder, desperately trying to reach up to the vaulted ceiling beams with a feather duster. After that, Shonda double-checked that housecleaners were written into the Church's budget as well. This meant that now, instead of battling her list of chores, her mother struggled with how to fill her days. Grace had become listless. This was just the second level of disappointment Shonda had been feeling lately in regard to her mother. The woman had often had hobbies or friends of her own, but lately she seemed detached. Sometimes now, her eyes were often lost out the window. She had to be "snapped out of it" often. It was cute for a little bit, just her growing a little older (although she looked 10 years younger than her true age) and spacey, but recently Shonda's investigative hackles were up. She was starting to suspect that something was up with her mother... and that was *before* her husband had been suddenly charged with murder.

Carrying all of this inside, Shonda showed none of it to the outside world. Brice had no idea he was walking next to a woman whose nerves were pulsing, stomach churning as she took the stairs and turned the ornate brass handle to pull open the massive front door. No, Brice thought she was the epitome of absolute cool. Beneath her powersuit, Shonda was anything but.

The Mountaintop shuttles out front had teed her up enough, so Shonda wasn't surprised – nor happy – to find that the Church's board of directors had already arrived and beaten her to her own mother's side. They were doing a mixture of consoling... and trying to find out who they could blame for the situation. It was all led by Deacon Stokes, a man who Shonda had grown to consider synonymous with evangelistic contempt. He had a way of looking down on people – both believers and non-believers – with a sneer that betrayed that he felt true salvation lay with him, not the Lord he claimed to serve. He was a completely self-centered man, though he extended his sense of self to Mountaintop Church as well. Any blemish on its record was considered a blemish on himself as well. It had taken him years to recover his fragile self-esteem after the scandal with the last pastor. He could be seen visibly shaking during services for months after. Shonda could tell, now that a new – and far more murderous – scandal was threatening a second beloved pastor, he planned to get out ahead of it like a politician's campaign manager covering up an affair.

Stokes was actually down on one knee, almost like he was proposing. He was bent before her mother – acting subservient, shocked, and 'there for her' – with the owl-like intensity of a predator behind his stare that let Shonda know that her mother was being interrogated: "Grace, who was this man? The dead man? Do you have any idea how Pastor Sherman knew him?" Shonda had interviewed enough clients and witnesses to know when questions were leading… when there were answers hoped for that the questions were being sculpted to provide. "Had the two of you received any suspicious mail of late, Grace? Threats or complaints? A great man like your husband can earn enemies. Do you think this could have anything to do with the neighboring churches?" He gave an aghast look during this last question – practically clutching pearls that he wasn't wearing (though Shonda had her suspicions that he wanted to). Having heard enough, she shut down this round of questioning with an authoritative voice that sounded just like she was shouting to the judge… which was just what Stokes was enjoying himself acting like.

"Motion to suppress, your honor! Leading the witness!"

Stokes gave a tiny, feeble jump at the sharp sting of her voice and Shonda gave little effort to stifle the smile this gave her – *Mission Accomplished*. The Deacon stood immediately, waving an arm to her mother as if to signal that he was allowing Shonda access. "Why, I didn't see you come in! This is no courtroom, my dear Shonda."

"You could have fooled me. Why don't you and the rest of the Mountaintop brigade head off and let me talk to my mother. She'll address any of your concerns when it's responsible to do so." At this, her mother looked up with a perplexed expression that worried Shonda for a moment – it was well within her power to tell the representatives of the Church that they were welcome to stay. Shonda hung on those next words, and was disappointed to hear, "You're not my lawyer. You're my daughter." For a frustrating moment, Deacon Stokes straightened his tie and got ready to return to his knee, but thankfully her mother still had *some* sense of what she really needed in this moment, "But she's right. I think I could use some time to myself."

At that, Shonda clapped her hands together repeatedly – sounding obnoxious and authoritative at the same time, making sure the Church Board got the message fast and clear. "Everyone who is not a member of this family get out of this house right now!" The board didn't like that, especially as Shonda picked up a decorative bowl from the table and started to beat it like a drum, driving them out like snakes. "Out out out! Go on now!"

As the rest of the Church board hurried out, Deacon Stokes scowled at her. "We own this house, you know."

Shonda didn't miss a beat. "Then I'm sure you don't want a crime scene here in the front hallway." He hated to be treated in such a way, and his eyes burned at her for a beat. Eventually, however, he was forced to demur, helping to clear the house as Brice showed him and the others to their cars.

It wasn't until the door closed that Shonda heard the charged whispers from nearby. She followed them to find her Aunts – Beth and Beverly – who were both huddled safely in the tea room. "Really? Having tea while your sister is getting the runaround?"

Beth's jaw dropped, not appreciating being talked to in such a way at all. "We came as soon as we heard, but the Deacon was already here." Beverly nodded in agreement. "We just want to help Grace whatever way we-"

"Then just stop talking. Give Mom some silence and help me keep any vultures like Stokes well enough away." She didn't wait to watch them register outrage, instead stepping quickly to her mother's side and offering her a hand. "I think? What you need right now? Is just some time to think. Don't you?" Without even looking up, her mother nodded. Her eyes were staring across the pristine white of the too-immaculate carpet, almost like she was trying to measure the inches of this immense room… always losing count. She had never been able to keep up with this infernal mansion.

Shonda sat with her mother and gave her exactly what she could tell she needed: *silence*. The two women felt small as they sat together in the middle of this gigantic living room, as fragile as the porcelain figurines on the side tables that Grace has collected all her life. So tiny in this massive house. She had never felt like her mother was happy here. Pastor Sherman was a good man – she could sense it, a true man of God, not a murderer – but this house… it had always been wrong for Mom. It was like she was stifled by the size of it. Buried under an avalanche of superfluous sitting rooms. After a while, Shonda reached for her mother's hand and – even after that – gave her mother silent companionship as their minds churned to process what had happened.

That silence was eventually broken as Beth and Beverly entered. The lack of gossip had become deafening to them, and they were eager to get to slather their opinions all over the tragedy. It had never been like either of them to sit out from a topic that needed their breathless input – anything from Shonda's love life to the color of the Mountaintop's new pews was fair game – and now they saw their opportunity to become a voice in this situation as well. Shonda knew that any input they would have in a serious situation like this would be ill-advised. She even caught herself thinking, "Jesus, anything. They can ask me as many questions about ex-boyfriends as they want. Just leave them out of this, okay?" Sometimes, however, Shonda had certainly learned that God says no. This was one of those times. Beth and Beverly came bearing tea for Grace, trying to keep up the appearance that they only wanted to care for her.

Shonda took a deep inhale and decided to give the women the benefit of the doubt. It was also worth noting that, not for nothing, Beverly made the most delicious Peach Tea that she had ever tasted in her life. She could remember staying at her house for an extra hour, surviving an onslaught of questions about "what dating was like nowadays... and as a working woman up on your high horse like that!?!" – all for the sake of a second helping of that tea serving up. She took a glass and melting with the first sip made her realize how much tension she was carrying. To think that, just this morning – mere hours ago – she woke just thinking it was going to be a "normal day" of bearing the stress of having to win a major court case. Now that mole hill of an event was being buried under a mountain of murder and family strife: *yeah, girl, maybe you could use a couple sips of tea... maybe it's not a bad thing that Beth and Beverly are here—*

– and then the onslaught of awful questions began. The moment the tea was set down. Right when Shonda's mouth was full and savoring for her first moment of relaxation of the day, they went right back to revealing their true colors by starting into a litany of questions and suspicions of their own. "Did you ever suspect that man was capable of such a thing, Grace?" "Did he ever hurt you?" "Was he a violent man? You can tell us." They didn't seem to take a stop to even breathe between sentences, catapulting from one terrible leap to another. "It must have been a crime of passion in some way." "Gosh, do you think he was in love with this man?" "Is he gay!?!"

Shonda set down her tea with a fierce enough clink to quiet them all. She cleared her throat, looking from one to the other – her mother's sisters who had always been there for her in times of both tragedy and joy, but never without this sense of gossip, self-service, and overdramatic jumping to conclusions. "Stop this right now! What a couple of old crows. You've both already jumped to the conclusion that he's guilty, is that it? And gay? Settle down. I think the man is innocent." That next moment spoke volumes to Shonda. Both Beth and Beverly clucked their tongues and eyed her with a wry sense of doubt: *really?*

Her mother remained quiet – she had been so still throughout all of this, hands shaking, clearly overcome with the awful news of the day. For the first time, Shonda felt how alone she was – not physically, but in opinion. It dawned on her that, of the four of them, *she was the only one whose instinct said that her stepfather was innocent.* That shook her faith mightily, but she snapped out of it, never one for not speaking her mind. "We need to find out what *really* happened. That's why I'm here. And that's why I visited him today."

This revelation gave the other women pause. Even her mother broke from her frozen position to look up at her, searching her eyes. "You saw him? How is he?" *There it was*, Shonda was relieved to think to herself, *there's my mother's compassion for her own husband.* "He's... holding up decently, all things considering. I've met many people in his situation in my line of work." Beth couldn't help but shift in her seat at this – Shonda having a high-end job, or any job at all, had always been a sticking point in their stuck-in-the-past minds. Sometimes it made Shonda wonder where she had actually come from. How did she grow into such a driven woman under the watch of such uninspiring women? Perhaps it was her generation. Maybe the death of her father. Whatever had made

Shonda who she was, that change was paying dividends today. Her reveal that she had spent an actual visit with her stepfather shut her lazy aunts up on the spot, trumping any snarky comments they had in mind about Shonda actually making something of herself.

Showing up her aunts was far from Shonda's actual to-do list today, though. The only woman she genuinely wanted to communicate with was her mother. She squeezed Grace's hand as she saw her eyes lift to hear more, inspired by sensing any feeling coming from the woman at all. "Mom, the only thing he had to say to me was that he didn't do this."

Grace's lip quivered. "And you believe him?" All three women looked at Grace at this, trying to discern what was going on in the mind of this beleaguered wife – *did she?*

"Yes, Mom. Of course I do."

Beth's voice was deadpan as she said what came next. It was the most serious Shonda had ever heard her. "But do you believe him because, as a lawyer, you think he's telling the truth? Or because, as a daughter, you *want him to be?*" Her aunt knew nothing about the instincts of a lawyer, but she knew she was asking a good question... and it was one that was actually haunting Shonda in her core. She was picking where to show her vulnerability today, however, and these women hadn't earned the privilege of seeing that they were getting under her skin. "I'm his *step*daughter," she quickly snapped, "and it doesn't matter what I think. What I need now – what Pastor Sherman needs – is proof. We don't have any yet. Just a pile of unfortunate questions that need answering." Both of her aunts pursed their lips, then Beverly murmured, "True. Very true. All I mean is... I'm just worried when you ask all of those questions... you might not like the answers you find." It made Shonda wonder – *was* she too close to this case to be objective? Might it be a disservice to the man, and her mother, for her to take the case on herself? The truth was that there was no time to worry about that now. There was only time to try and make all of this right.

A sad surprise was ahead of Shonda now, though. Her instinct had led her to believe that, of all people, her mother would be the most relieved to have her help in the matter. Surely she would be her greatest ally in exonerating her stepfather? It turned out that, this time, her instinct was all wrong. The tension with her sisters, the Church board, and the possibility of being married to a murderer was just too much for her for the day. Without a sound, she patted Shonda's hand, sat up, and rose – still silent – to cross the room and head down one of the expansive hallways. Shonda felt like she watched her walking away for an eternity. Taking step by step out of the conflict. It was too much for Grace to bear. She entered her bedroom, closing the door behind her. The cold click of the knob's lock – tiny and distant – fired like a gunshot right into Shonda. If she was looking for a hand to hold through all of this, it wasn't going to be her mother's.

That day Shonda learned that it was possible to have too much of her aunt's Peach Tea. They sat there in vigil for hours. Beth nervously dusted the piano, the collectibles, everything... not caring that it was all clean in the first place. Beverly also wasted her time doing unnecessary chores, picking tiny specs of lint from the carpet or licking her finger to smudge out fingerprints from the window. Even the tiniest of sounds echoed out in the expansive room. It felt like they were sitting shiva, mourning a dead person. Well, Shonda thought, someone *is* dead. And *that* is what someone needs to do something about. And that someone? Was her. These women were obviously planning on staying inside here, alone together, with no idea what the fate of Pastor Sherman would be (but with every intention of gossiping about the possibilities). They were wondering if he was even the man they all thought they knew in the first place. Shonda needed to know firsthand. Eventually, she just couldn't take the inaction any longer. "Being there for her mother" was starting to feel like joining her in defeat and despondency. So it was time for her to rise. She marched down the long hallway and gave a soft knock. "Mom? I'm leaving." She listened for any response… but knew she would receive none. Instead, she laid out what was going to happen. "Mom. I'm going to go now. I'm going to get out of this house and go and fix this." At this, she heard only a tiny murmur from inside. With the sharp dutiful nod of a daughter with an unimaginable mission, she turned and left – intent that she would not return without some answers.

It was a mission she thought that she was now on alone, but outside…

… she was surprised to find Brice, still waiting on her, leaning up against the hood of his car. He had every chance to leave with the others from Mountaintop earlier, and yet here he was. With another guy, Shonda would have just assumed he was playing a mid to long game to get laid. It was a class move. Might have even worked. With Brice, however, she could tell there was a genuine desire, but it was hard for her to put an idea so foreign to her into words. It was plain on his face. He just wanted to be there for her. It was the type of sincerity she had rarely been shown by the opposite sex, though some often accused her of not being able to recognize it when it was right in front of her. Her aunts liked to accuse her of dating a long list of guys who treated her like dirt. They weren't wrong, no matter how much she wished they were. Now, here she was with a guy that wore the best of intentions on his sleeve and – classic Shonda – she had no idea how to deal with it. So she defaulted to a nice, sharp and detached sense of snark.

"What are you trying to be? My chauffeur for the worst day of my life?" He managed a smile, but she could tell he wasn't sure how much humor she was looking to blend into this awful day.

"Something like that. Listen, I'm– I'm just seeing what you're going through, is all. My family– and, hell, myself– I've been through my share of–"

"Murder raps?"

He scoffed and looked to his feet; she found it kind of cute that she was able to disarm him so easily. "No, not murder raps, I suppose. But still. Just seems to me, after seeing everything you've got going on around you, what you really need is for someone to…" She cocked an eyebrow, *just where was this guy heading with this?* His kind and eager candor took her aback. "I think what you need is someone here to help not hinder." The phrasing stopped her. Their eyes locked – it reminded her, for an instant, of the silent and important moment she spent with her mother – but there was something much more there of course, a spark of chemistry that might have led somewhere on a day that wasn't hell. In the meantime, she could tell he liked being able to disarm her as much as she had him moments ago.

Pleased with himself and happy to be of help, he opened the passenger door for her. She nodded with appreciation and hooked her legs to slide inside. Her smile curled a bit as she realized she was letting her skirt slide up her thigh just a touch more than necessary – a bit of a show for Prince Charming here. It gave her some girlish butterflies to flirt, even almost-imperceptibly, as a bit of a reprieve from everything that was going on. Whatever their future – just as friends, or with benefits involved along the way – it was nice to have him here.

"That… is actually *exactly* what I need. Well then, Worst Day Chauffer – to my office! I need to prep my people for–" The next words caught in her throat as she said them, realizing the truth in them, "I need their help to win the most important case of my life."

On the way, Brice watched as Shonda stared out the window – lost in thought. Every few blocks, a new text from her legal team would send her into a flurry of finger-tapping on her phone. "Geeze, you text faster than I drive." She smiled at this, showing off a bit but – once she hit reply – her eyes drifted back out to the horizon. He hazarded to check in. "You alright?" Off her look, he waved a hand, "I know. I know. Help not hinder. Just needed to ask, okay?"

She patted his knee, "Thanks. I get it. I'm okay. This can't be about me. I won't let it be about me. It's… I'm thinking more of my Mom."

Brice nodded and drove on, deciding not to pry further. Flirting aside, Shonda genuinely felt comfortable around him, and found herself needing to talk out some of her feelings. "This is just the last thing a woman like my mom needs – not that any woman wants a husband who may-or-may-not be a murderer – it's just… Sherman was supposed to be different, but the guy I talked to today was– he was troubled. I can't say guilty, just, haunted, you know? But what I can't wrap my brain around is… why wouldn't he talk to me? He must be protecting someone."

Brice gave a deep sigh of understanding. "No offense, but it sounds like maybe you should let this case 'be about you' at least a little bit." She let that sink in with a nod, but was relieved she didn't need to answer that as they rolled in to park outside of her law firm.

CHAPTER THREE

As Brice pulled into the parking circle of Kerns & Dunaway, and Shonda saw Terrance Dunaway already outside to meet them in the courtyard, she could tell that he was having his own concerns. Without a word, he held his arms wide, anticipating her needing comfort. She stepped out of the car, stared right into those open arms, and stopped in her tracks. "Terrance, I– I don't think that's a good idea."

His arms lowered, eyes growing even more distressed, "Shonda, I'm going to insist that you not go through all of this alone." Brice cleared his throat next to her and Terrance looked to him. "Oh, who are–"

Shonda broke in. "This is Brice. He works at the church and delivered the news to me this morning."

Brice shook his hand. "I've kind of been her chauffeur ever since, but it's my pleasure. Reverend Sherman means a great deal to me as well."

With that, Shonda chirped, "So you see? I'm not alone. But, for at least a while, I'd like to be. So please keep everyone out of my office." Then she sidestepped past Terrance to get inside as quickly as possible.

Terrance had a well of empathy that knew no bounds. He knew when a person, especially one he cared about, wasn't allowing themselves to express their feelings. It was the kind of soft heart that many lawyers mistakenly took for a weakness in the man at first, but with Terrance it was more like he could see right into a person's heart... a terrifying concept for a guilty criminal or a lying witness. In Shonda's case, however, it was a slight annoyance in times like these. His loving care was a fierce challenge when she was desperately trying to keep herself together.

It was that intense sympathy that powered Terrance as he marched right inside after Shonda, even as she tried to escape him. "Now, my girl, please listen to me. If I think you're too close to this thing, I have every right to make sure you don't work this case in any way. I can't have you hurt by—"

She raised a hand and stopped him, using a careful moment of silence to let Terrance know that he was appreciated, noticed, and should just drop it. It was risky to shush her boss like that – not every lawyer at the firm would be able to do so, you don't just 'shush' Terrance – but Shonda was special and desperate times called desperately for him to stop talking. He abided by her silent request, and followed her into the building. Brice smirked as he hurried after. Though he didn't know Terrance, he read the tense emotions and electricity in the air between the two professionals and knew very well that he should stay quiet too.

Inside, Shonda could see her team of assistants already hard at work in the central workspace. Its open plan always made it very possible to see where others were and, sometimes, what they were doing from across the building. All in the name of Terrance's quest for transparency and calm. Shonda probably could have guessed what her team was already doing, even without seeing them. In other circumstances, she probably would have let herself feel a swell of pride that she had trained them so well. There they were – pouring over law books, searching for similar cases with precedents they could use to their advantage and gathering information on Pastor Sherman and the victim. It was just like she had taught them. At the sound of her heels clicking into the front lobby of the building, the entire team had stopped and looked across at her. They had a healthy fear of her, and often looked like deer in headlights as she stepped in, even when they were doing a great job. This time, however, it was Shonda who felt like a deer: *was there anyone in this building that didn't want to stare at her until she cried?* She stood her ground and could tell the team didn't know what to do. Usually she would approach. Bravely, a couple of them started towards her. Instantly, Shonda instead clicked those heels right over to the stairs and made her way up to her second floor private office – which right now felt more like a sanctuary.

The soft click of the door locking behind her was the sweetest sound Shonda had heard all day – or perhaps ever. Brice had been a (quite handsome) knight in shining armor – keeping her company ever since delivering her the awful news of the day – but it had meant that she hadn't had a moment to herself until right now. She didn't feel the need to cry, just to be still and silent and in control of her surroundings. She looked around the office and was amazed at how normal and unaffected everything was. Didn't the tiny, fragile decorations on her desk and bookshelves know that the world had been torn upside-down today? Didn't her awards realize that her entire psyche was spinning? No, her belongings were all the same in this new post-tragedy world. Her diploma hung right where it always was, seeming to ask Shonda if she was good enough for what was coming.

She slid into her high-backed leather chair and let it spin. Not fast, just a few soft circles pushed on by soft taps of her heel or her fingertips pushing off the dark mahogany of her desk. Shonda didn't let her clients ever see how much she liked to spin in her expensive chair. It brought back the kid in her – many memories of visiting her biological father's office. He had been a file clerk and was probably ashamed by the tiny office but, to her, it had been a secret wonderland – mostly because it had a chair that spun. She used to watch her buckle shoes spin around as she kicked against his rickety file cabinets. What would he have thought to see her stupid-big office and ridiculously large desk that was probably the size of that tiny file clerk office of his, that she remembered so fondly?

It was ironic that it was now – as always – completely covered in papers. "I keep a clean record but a messy desk…" she had said to the cleaning service when she started to work there, "… so you don't need to ever touch anything on it." The cleaners had respected that rule, and the office usually looked spic and span and spotless… all around a mahogany island of towering piles of papers.

Her mother had tutted at the fact that it was cleaned by a service and not her own elbow grease. "You shouldn't be making women clean your office."

Shonda had tutted her right back. "Shows what you know, Mom. Our cleaning lady… is a man!" Usually after winning a case, like she had just this morning, she spun herself extra fast as a tiny, silly reward. Today, however, she could only bring herself to give herself a slow turn, staring at the walls around her. Empty and sad.

Then she stopped spinning. Her eyes rested on her purse on the desk, suddenly remembering what was inside. She softly pulled it open and there it was: the pencil cup she had been given by her client's daughter, Jessica, that morning. The oddly colored object looked so funny inside her Gucci purse. It seemed to speak, "Thank you for saving my Mom." It was a dazzle of glitter and unicorn stickers, a complete contrast to Shonda's room. She pulled the cup out and placed it beside her nameplate. Looking around her desk, she picked up all the various pens and pencils nested in the piles and dropped them all – *ting, ting, tok* – into the tiny metal tin.

She let out a gasp as she realized that she had a *new*, cherished pencil to add to the cup as well – the one that she had waited to see if Juror #3 would pick up in the case to exonerate Jessica's mother. Shonda had made it a point to collect that pencil from the juror's box as a tiny little trophy, joking in her head how funny it would be to have to pay a fine for stealing county property. With a soft snap of her fingers, she sent the new pencil clicking into the cup. Even though it still vaguely smelled of chicken soup, filling it gave her a soothing, satisfying feeling, especially when adding a pencil that signified her success from earlier in the day. "Thank you, Jessica. I needed that."

Her name on the side in magic marker made her smile warmly. It was spelled incorrectly but it was spectacular. Seeing that rainbow *'Shawnduh'* across the side gave her a childlike moment of peace even more than her usual chair spins.

Back downstairs, Terrance and Brice were coping with the awkwardness of being strangers suddenly left alone together. Terrance led him over to the office's snack area. "So, you work for the Pastor?"

Brice nodded as he warmed his face with a coffee, eyes growing distant as he thought of the man. "He means a great deal to me too. He's my rock, nothing I wouldn't do for him." Terrance agreed that he was a good man, or at least he thought he was. This made Brice consider him for a moment before asking, "Are you a Christian?"

To this, Terrance shook his head. "No, I'm a parishioner of the law room." He swallowed hard as he considered that. "But I have faith in that church as well. Cases like your pastor's tend to shake it something awful." The idea landed on both of them hard, worried about the days ahead and what revelations were ready to come.

Back upstairs, Shonda watched her team below through a window into the common workspace. Such busy bees, and their activity was almost a balm to her frayed nerves. She decided it was time to pull her head out of the sand and rejoin the universe – if anything was going to save her stepfather, it would need her at the helm. She stepped towards the door and gave a wince as her ankle rubbed raw in her cherished red heels. She looked down at her feet. She'd been wearing them all day. Commonly, on a trial day, she would have removed them immediately after getting back to the car and slipped on her simple black Rothys – a matching pair of which were waiting comfortably for her under the desk. They meant more than just comfort, however. She wasn't sure if anyone had ever noticed, but those black comfortable shoes were also what she wore to the courthouse if she believed she was going to lose her case. Or if she was struggling to defend someone she felt was guilty. Her eyes moved back and forth between the soft black Rothys and her tight, perfect red "success" heels. Though her feet ached to change, her superstition was too much. She stepped to the door with the same sharp heel taps that these exact shoes rang out in the courtroom earlier, trying to control her whimper of pain as they dug into her ankle. She looked to Jessica's pencil cup on the desk one last time. How she hoped for a similar victory for her stepfather as well. If she could win this one, however, she wouldn't need a child-decorated trophy for it. All she wanted was her family back.

Downstairs, the room was buzzing with activity. Shonda wasn't surprised – she had a strong team that had only grown stronger under her instruction and the mentorship of Terrance – but she also noticed a remarkably different energy with this case. She could tell that was because they all knew how personal it was for her. One of her interns, Meredith, was always the first to brief Shonda. She was the teacher's pet of the group if ever there was one, assuming that bravely taking on the job of communication with their boss would help her rise in Shonda's esteem. Shonda smirked thinking: *You know what? She's right.* Meredith *was* Shonda's favorite, probably because of her go-getter courage about bringing Shonda any news, good or bad. She was the first Shonda had in mind for promoting. Today, however, even Meredith was nervous about approaching her to talk about her findings…

… so, this time, Shonda stepped to her. "Okay, catch me up."

Nothing goosed Meredith like a good set of marching orders. Her face was animated as she laid out what they knew. "Okay, the victim is a Marshall Cooper at 4201 South Point Circle. Originally from New Jersey. He's a former construction worker who made his way up in the business, eventually becoming his own boss and hiring teams of his own to work on his own designs. He's responsible for a number of projects around the city, Shonda. Everything from MARTA stations to a section of the Midtown Union. He helped when they added a new ward to the prison and beat out a ton of competition to win the contract for that ornate new square down by the riverfront. I've been scouring every method but finding no connection between Mr. Cooper and y– your– Pastor Sherman. I promise to keep looking."

Meredith wasn't the only one having trouble vocalizing her findings. Even as they performed well and answered her questions, the team all tended to avoid eye contact with her, probably because they were unsure how well she was keeping up. In order for this to work, Shonda was going to have to address the elephant in the room. "Hey, guys? Listen. I know you know what this case means to me. But it's still me here. I don't want any pussyfooting with the facts or sugarcoating. That won't get us anywhere. As of today, I am investigating Reverend Sherman Richards–" she paused, finding the words insincere and catching in her throat. "I'm investigating my stepfather – Dad – in a case of murder in the first degree. To do that, I need to also let it go and lock in like I would any case. We all do. The best way you can help me is to hit it as hard as I know the best team in the city can." They all seemed to breathe a sigh of genuine relief to hear her talk about it. "I mean it. Whatever we find, I want you to tell me – good or bad." With a renewed vigor, her people got to work.

Even without the personal connection, it was a tricky and unique case. Even beyond the letter in his handwriting being found inside the victim's mouth, there were other signs pointing to the possibility that Pastor Sherman had, in fact, committed the crime. His schedule was uncharacteristically empty on the night of the murder. For any man in charge of such a megachurch, every square of the calendar was often filled and bursting with meetings and events. For Pastor Sherman, it was even more so. He prided himself on penciling in personal meetings with as many church members as he could. A pillar of his church was real check ins with members young and old. It was a true selling point of Mountaintop. Newcomers were often shocked out of their socks to find Pastor Sherman on their doorstep with a coffee cake in hand even after visiting the church only one or two times. He was considered a man who knew how to find people. Every time he made one of those visits, however, it was dutifully penciled into his schedule. This resulted in a personal calendar that looked like Grand Central Station. It resembled the agenda of two or three men, all rolled into one. But on that night, the night Marshall Cooper was killed, Pastor Sherman had no plans. It was the only night of that month with any room on the docket. The emptiness of the calendar square ached with suspicion. Furthermore, a program for a recent service at Mountaintop Church was found on the premises of the victim's house.

She surprised herself by her assuredness, and worried herself a bit too. In any other case, she wouldn't be as assuming – as her words obviously made it clear she was – that her client was innocent. This morning's victory for Jessica's mother could be a part of why she was feeling a bit cocky, sure, but that was overcome by a concern that her relationship with the accused here could be clouding her judgment. She shook away self-doubt, however, knowing the only answer was to address the case as she would any other. She had to ask the same questions she would if she were investigating a total stranger. "If the prosecution can't find any connection between Pastor Sherman and Mr. Cooper as well, then they're going to need a good strong motive. There's evidence that he did it, sure, but why? Why would a man who preaches 'thou shalt not kill'… suddenly do so. And why *this* man in particular. Motive is a huge hole in the story here. Our only counter to the prosecution coming up with one will be finding it for ourselves too."

This notion was met with nods all around. The entire team regarded each other with silent purpose, which was suddenly broken by the sound of... "*What a Fool Believes*," by The Doobie Brothers. Everyone in the room looked over to an alcove, where Terrance eyed the pocket of Brice, who jumped and said, "Oh, that's me."

As he fumbled for his phone, Terrance commented, "Well it's certainly none of us. You're a Doobie Brother's fan?" The room laughed, especially as Terrance continued as Brice unsnapped a flip phone, "and you have a flip phone?" Shonda smirked as Brice took his call, silencing Michael McDonald's voice from echoing throughout the room. He had such a strength and self-assurance, but it was often made more human by what a strange dork the guy was – with tastes which some might mistake for being old-fashioned or out-of-touch, but she preferred to consider as bizarrely unique.

There was no humor, only urgency, when he snapped his flip phone shut again. He stepped to Shonda, car keys already in his hand, and cleared his throat. "I think we should go. Now. Deacon Stokes just called an emergency meeting of Mountaintop's Board of Directors. I have a feeling that you'll want to–" but she was already moving past him for the doors. He finished his sentence to Terrance. "Yeah. She's going to want to be there."

Terrance took his arm as he started to follow her. "Watch over her. We'll do everything we can here. And Brice... thank you for being with her. A faith like yours might be able to move the mountains we need."

Meredith smiled. "Though, while you're at it, maybe update your cell phone – and the ring – sometime."

Before Brice could defend himself, Shonda was sounding the call from the door. "Come on, Brice! We have to be there for that meeting. Let's go!"

Brice's foot was noticeably harder on the gas as they sped to the church. Shonda could tell, as she suspected too, that Brice was suspicious of the Mountaintop board members making the wrong moves in this situation, left unchecked and acting out of fear. "There are a million wrong plays your board could make here, firing the Pastor before trial could make him look even guiltier in the public eye – that stigma could cloud a jury. They could hang an innocent man by trying to do the right thing. Lord knows I've seen the board blow it in the name of the Lord before."

Brice spoke up, making sure she was careful. "Hey, I agree, we gotta get there to set 'em right. But those men are good men, acting for the good of the church body. They've just never had to face something like this. Believe me, I know when leadership goes criminal. These guys have hubris, but they're not corrupt."

Shonda immediately felt bad about the shade she had thrown on the church leaders. "I'm sorry. I didn't mean that. Stokes has just… riled me up in the past, that's all."

Brice made sure to qualify what he had meant. "Whoa whoa whoa, listen. I know the guy can be a bit of a… complete disaster too." They both laughed at this. "I was there at your Mom's this morning, remember?"

She rolled her eyes. "Gosh, was that only this morning?" They both let the tense moment flow under the bridge. Shonda regarded Brice. He was a good man, and easy to talk to. She let herself push to learn more about him. "You said you know about when leadership goes criminal. Is that the kind of thing that made you choose to leave the force?"

Brice drove on in silence for a while, trying to figure out how much to say. "The short answer is yes, but perhaps sometime I can give you the long one. It's not something I share with too many people. The memories are unpleasant and I'm not one to talk about it. That okay?" It was his turn to be the emotionally scarred one in the car.

Shonda certainly understood what it was to not want to talk about your pain. "Of course. We don't have to talk about it if you don't want to. What was it you said? 'Only here to help, not hinder?' "

This earned a smile from Brice, who realized that he didn't open up much to others about his past. There was something about this woman, however, that made him know he could speak from the heart. "We can talk about what happened to me after I left though? If you like?"

She nodded. "Anything you like."

His manner changed as he started to think about a tougher period in his life. "You know I fought long and hard with myself about leaving the force. It was killing the dream. I wanted to wear a badge ever since I was a kid. Stopping the bad guys. Being a hero. Like you were getting at, I started finding out that some of my heroes were the bad guys. I quit after I couldn't take it anymore, but what does a police officer do for a living once he's no longer police? It was hard to find work after that. Employers love to hire retired police because they know they're trustworthy and capable... but a guy who quit the force? What's that about? They all wanted to know the story, but I wasn't going to rat on the Chief of Police just to get a job as a mall cop. So my loyal silence made me suspicious. Ironically, I had taken a stand that made people stop trusting me."

She sighed as she considered what a shame that was, but liked it when she heard Brice suddenly laugh. "Oh wow, we're passing it now. See that family restaurant over there?" He pointed to a bright green building with cartoon characters painted all over it. She knew the place well.

"That's Gil the Gopher's! It's got those robot animals that sing to you while you eat. It's such a Chuck E. Cheese rip off, but I used to love going there as a kid."

Brice smiled. "I did too. Then, one day, I was running out of options. I even applied there." They both laughed at this, and Shonda was confused.

"You applied to be a talking animal?"

He gave her a playful punch to the shoulder. "No, I applied to be security, smart-aleck." Then his manner darkened even more. "They turned me down. That was the last place that told me in so many words that they didn't trust me. *That* place. Where I had kicked around in the ball pool when I was five. It was heavy to be turned down by such a place… and felt real bad to break down in their parking lot."

She could tell this was a painful memory, and stayed quiet as he continued, "So there I was, weeping at my lowly state in my car outside Gil the Gopher's– don't laugh!" Shonda wasn't, and instead was deeply invested in him revealing such personal memories. "And I swear, here's how it happened, I looked out my windshield through tears, up this hill I'm turning into right now… and here it was." Sure enough, as he turned there it was on the top of the hill: Mountaintop Church. "I saw the cross up here on the top of the hill and I began to pray. I prayed for direction. For purpose. And, heck, for a way to just pay the rent. I had heard the church was under new leadership and I drove up here and asked if they needed help." As he remembered this part of the story, his eyes brightened. "That's when Pastor Sherman took me in. I was at the end of my rope. Flailing for a place that would take me. When he offered me a gig being security for Mountaintop, I thought it was a joke but… it changed me." There was a moment of silence as he thought about the charges that were being leveled at his leader and what that meant for him, "I guess I have a lot of me invested in this too. I believe in him. Because he believed in me. Because of that, there's nothing I wouldn't do for him. I owe the man my life."

CHAPTER FOUR

When they arrived at Mountaintop, the entire church campus was humming with tension. Where usually there were bright faces waiting to greet newcomers and visitors, now were worried faces fearful of what was to come. Brice was shocked that the parking lot was host to three separate news vans. "How are they here already?"

Shonda was sadly used to it. "That's their job. And they're very good at it. Get moving, we have to get inside. The church's response to them could be part of the problem."

She rushed inside just as news reporters were being turned away by Kyle Sheffield, the Junior Pastor at Mountaintop. He was *not* used to handling the press and was making a true mess of it. "Enough with this persecution! We here at Mountaintop know even less than you do about any of this!"

An intrepid and eager reporter shoved her microphone right up to Sheffield's face as she asked, "Do you consider your pastor a murderer, sir?"

Sheffield stammered awkwardly, and his stuttered answer sounded frightened and uncertain. "Of course not! I don't think– I mean, who can know– the accusations are very serious and we here at Mountaintop trust our police to act appropriately– should he be guilty – OR NOT! I mean, of course not–"

Shonda tugged the microphone out of his face and practically leaped in front of him, bearing the full brunt of the cadre of bright lights and microphones that the news crews rabidly pivoted right at her. "I'll be acting as legal counsel for Sherman Richards and I ask that the press give the man and his family – and workplace – the privacy in this matter they would expect for themselves."

The reporters didn't like the sound of that, barking at her, "That would all be fine and good, but this man is a leader to many – he's a public figure. And what's your name?"

One of the other reporters knew her name just fine, however, and was delighted to reveal it and its juicy connotations. "Shonda *Lassiter*, isn't it? Stepdaughter of the accused, aren't you? How would you like me to spell 'conflict of interest' in my article? I'm sure my readership will have a lot to say about you being the representative on this case."

The issue was rudely stated, but the reporter wasn't wrong. Shonda paused in the face of the question – *a good one*, she knew. Sometimes, however, the best answer to aggressive questioning was a swift kick out the door. The reporter shot her a cocky "gotcha" smirk, thinking she had Shonda right where she wanted her. Turns out she was way wrong. On a dime, Shonda raised an eyebrow and gave them all their walking papers instead. "Oh, I'm sorry, were you waiting for an answer? We called no press conference and you are on private grounds at the mercy of the church, which respectfully ask for you to get off of it. I have security here if that will be a problem?" She nodded to Brice, who smiled at this and stepped forward, on cue, puffing his powerful chest and lifting a strong arm to the door.

"Right this way, if you will?" As they filed out, Brice and Shonda admired each other – they were learning to like working together, but also being by each other's side as well. "That was pretty amazing, watching you tell them to get out with such class."

Before she even knew what she was saying, she found herself flirting back a response. "Well, it helps to have a guy next to me with arms like yours. She probably thought you were going to lay hands on her. Who knows? Might have been hoping so."

Wait, what was that!?!

Brice smirked at her little complimentary joke. He liked it, but brushed it off. Shonda, however, was deeply embarrassed. That kind of flirt was common to many, but it was the most overtly "come hither" thing she had said in years. She was *not* known for being open to romantic winks to the opposite sex. Her honest but desperate climb up the ladder at her law firm had been built upon sticking to her guns and not using her sex as any part of her resume. Those around her did consider her beautiful (she had been told, anyway) and sometimes would act on it, even asking her out if their work relationship made the idea inappropriate. Her constant rebuffs, however, had earned her a reputation as a bit of an ice queen.

Terrance had told her not to be ashamed of that – to instead wear it like a badge of honor. "Believe me, I know how the women who work at the opposite end of the extreme end up. You will too. Their cuckolded spouses usually end up as our clients… and those cases are easily won." Here she was, however – "The Ice Queen" – blushing like a schoolgirl in the church lobby, telling her musclebound friend that she liked his physique?

She looked to the floor awkwardly. The moment – to her – seemed to drag on for an eternity, until she was saved by Sheffield as he started to step away. "Thank you for that. I'm not used to speaking to cameras and news. Now, if you'll excuse me, we have an emergency meeting of the board of directors–"

"I know, that's why we're here." This stopped Sheffield. At first, he wasn't ready to allow an outsider, even the stepdaughter of the pastor, to be allowed into a session on such a sensitive topic. She asserted how important it was, however. "You're not used to cameras, right? Well, there are going to be plenty more coming. That was only the opening salvo. You and the board need to get a response ready and a social media plan in place to deal with all of this – as well as how to act while we find out who really killed that man."

This sent a shot through Sheffield. "Wait… did the pastor *not* kill that man?" It was as though he hadn't even thought of the happy possibility.

Shonda grabbed him by the arm and led him to the board's meeting room herself. "And *that* kind of doubt expressed in public is a great place for us to start. Come on. We have a ton to talk about and we'd better make it fast. A man's freedom and the reputation of this church depends on it."

The rest of the church board was just as uneasy as Sheffield had been to see Shonda enter this private emergency session. Once she heard some of their first instincts with how to deal with the problem, however, she was even happier that she had asserted herself. She was surprised to see another church member she barely knew, Virgil, sitting away from the long conference table and taking notes. She knew he happened to be a private investigator: *What's he doing here? That can't be good.* She took a seat at the table, shocked as she listened to how easily these men had already succumbed to the idea that their head pastor was a murderer, and a few of them were already very prepared to throw the man under the bus. "Shonda, you have to understand, it's for the good of the church. We're not going to fire him, heavens no, just… ask him to resign."

Shonda shot up out of her chair, rising above the board and smacking her fist into the wood. "This man needs you right now! He needs his church – his flock – to not give in to fear and stand behind him. Stop acting like he's guilty!"

From nearby, a quiet voice murmured the awful thought that was simmering in all of their minds. "Shonda. What if he *is* guilty?"

She shook her head. "We'll deal with that – and what it does to our hearts and souls, our family and church – once there's proof. Right now there is no evidence, not even a motive–"

At this idea, however, Shonda watched as Deacon Stokes (church fuddy duddy) gave a side eye to another.

It was more than a "she's crazy" look. It was the look of someone hiding something. She stepped around the table, pointed a finger, and asked a question she wasn't sure she wanted the answer to. "What don't I know? What was that look? What are you not telling me?" The board members sheepishly shrugged at first, but could tell they were caught. More murmurs started around the table. Shonda's head spun in all directions. "Wait, what are *all of* you not telling me?"

Sheffield spoke up from the end of the table. He hated what he now had to tell her. "Shonda, Pastor Sherman… your stepfather… had been going through some personal issues." She had no idea what he was about to tell her, but she felt a specter of dread loom throughout the room. "There was… some infidelity."

She bristled. It was beyond her ability to believe. "He cheated on my mom? And you're covering it up?"

Sheffield winced, but raised a finger. "No. It's not that. Not exactly. Virgil? We'd better show them the tapes."

What tapes?

Shonda's blood ran cold as Virgil rose and moved to a nearby television bay that was set up in the corner. He fiddled with the instruments until a picture came up… showing Pastor Sherman alone in his office. "What is this? You've been spying on him?" Shonda questioned.

Brice touched her shoulder. "That's a security feed the pastor knows about. It was his idea, actually. He always wanted full transparency – never for any corner of his church to be a place of secrets."

The idea seemed beautiful to Shonda, for just a moment, and then she got worried as she realized this act was about to lead her to seeing something the man didn't want revealed. "Wait, what are you about to show me?"

Sheffield nodded for Virgil to begin the tape. "Just watch."

On the screen, Pastor Sherman was on his knees in prayer. He let out a slow breath, the words barely audible as he whispered. The words of his prayer were peaceful, but Shonda worried that their underlying message was that her stepfather, indeed, had something to hide. "Was this taken after the murder?"

Still standing by the television, Virgil shook his head. "No, whoever killed Marshall Cooper, he's still very much alive when this tape was made. In fact, I had just visited your father that same day."

She started at this. "You had? Why?"

Virgil just nodded to the screen "Watch and you'll see."

On the television, a female voice buzzed in over the intercom. "Pastor Sherman?"

"Yes, Donna," Sherman answered.

"Virgil is here to see you. He said you're expecting him. However, I don't see any afternoon appointments on your calendar."

However, Sherman seemed to be making an effort to keep his cool here, though it was apparent that he sensed Donna's protective stance. He answered calmly, "I am expecting him. No worries. I simply kept it off of the books because it is dealing with a matter of great delicacy. If you will, show Virgil to my office please. Thank you."

"Yes, sir," she replied, in a more relaxed tone, and then quickly hung up the phone to do as he instructed her.

Within seconds, the office doors opened on screen, showing Virgil himself entering with a manila folder in hand. He looked emotional – a bearer of bad news. Sometimes, a private investigator carried a smarmy smirk when that was the case, but here Virgil seemed to be under a dark cloud himself. This was obviously bad news for both of them – but he was also determined, a man on a mission who wasn't one to suffer much small talk. You could tell he was taking his work very seriously, especially his latest assignment for his current client – who just so happened to be the pastor of his own church.

Sherman's hands were visibly shaking as he stood to greet him. He seemed on the brink of emotional devastation awaiting the results of Virgil's investigation. Shonda knew – as her stepfather must have as well – that Virgil was a highly recommended private investigator with a promise of excellence and no mistakes. He had a military background and an impeccable reputation. His clients sought after information that must be held in the strictest confidence. Virgil knew how to meet the needs of his select clientele, and Sherman apparently was now one of them. Donna closed the door behind her, leaving the two men alone. On the screen, Virgil looked right into the camera, casting a dubious eye to the fact that they were being taped. "Pastor, are you sure you want this recorded?" He asked him this with a tone that betrayed that he, himself, *very much* did not think it should be.

Sherman motioned for him to take a seat. "Of course. I want everything on the record, no improprieties, you know that. If I expect that kind of openness in others I must also demand it of myself."

Virgil shifted in his chair at this. "But, Pastor, there… there *have* been improprieties. And I want you protected."

"The Lord protects me, Virgil. Even from this. Especially this, actually, because it's a trial he has chosen for me – and all of us – to soldier through. And Corinthians 10… the Lord never puts us up to any trials that we cannot bear. You know that." Sherman rubbed his weary brow, a subtle show of nervousness, as he anticipated Virgil's news.

"I do. I know that only thanks to you."

Displaying a weak and forced half smile, Sherman said, "Right. Then let's get to it now. You have something for me?"

Shifting his weight in his chair, Virgil replied, "I do."

Virgil handed Sherman the manila folder that he immediately opened once it was in his hands. From the envelope, he pulled out a handful of large blown-up pictures. Shonda leaned in towards the screen, desperately trying to make out what the pictures contained. All she could see was her stepfather's sad eyes as he leafed through the photographs. After taking each one in, some with a longer gaze than others, he began to blink in disbelief. Heartbreak filled his face.

Shonda had seen guilt awash over the face of countless criminals during her career. She had also seen something else, however. The disappointing sadness, the grief that came when an innocent party was forced to stare at the proof that they had been wronged by someone they thought was their closest love. *That* was the inescapable expression that she now saw flood the face of this poor, troubled man. Even without seeing the photos herself, Shonda immediately knew by that look what the pictures were proof of, and her mouth said it aloud before her brain even considered whether it was a good idea…

"My mother was having an affair."

No one in the room needed to give her an answer.

Everyone in the room knew that she was right.

On screen, Virgil went on. "His name is Marshall Cooper. He lives at 4201 South Point Circle. She sees him around lunchtime on Tuesdays and Thursdays. She's there usually two or three hours at most." In light of Marshall Cooper's murder, hearing his name out loud in this context took on a haunting tone. Shonda closed her eyes with the awful realization. "And there's motive…"

"She's been lying to me," Sherman mumbled in the video. He was deflated and breaking down, the pain evident in his longing stare as Virgil went on.

"While you were at the Oakland conference last month, the Sunday she called in sick to the bible study she leads here, I can go on—"

"Okay. Okay, that's enough. Th– than–" There was a shudder of confusion in this polite man, not knowing whether to thank a person for this kind of life-changing bad news.

Virgil looked grief-stricken himself, delivering this information. "Pastor. I'm so sorry about this. So sorry you had to find out this way, sir. From me. It gives me no pleasure to use the tools at my disposal to uncover awful things like that about you."

The pastor took his hand. "About *her*, Virgil. I'm still here. The man you know, broken but un-bowed. And you just remember, those investigative skills of yours are a gift from God, no matter how soaked in the sins of the world they may seem at times." There was still the man they all knew, Pastor Sherman trying to comfort another even as his life spun out of control all around him. "None of this is your fault, Virgil. Don't be ridiculous. You did only what I asked and, Virgil? I know this seems odd to say but... th– thank you." There it was. As hard as it was for him to say, the man had to get it out.

Pastor Sherman's voice trailed off – the man was understandably having a hard time keeping it together. He remained quiet for a brief moment, almost lifeless. Then, with a quick inhale, as if he'd been brought back to life, he clapped Virgil on the back. "I appreciate the work you've done here. How much do I owe you?"

Virgil waved this off. "I could never. Not after everything you've done for me. I owe you my life... my salvation–"

Sherman clapped his back again at this, and this time there was some tough love to it. "No, Virgil, your salvation comes not from me. Not even from your own works. It comes from the Lord."

Nodding at this, but still refusing payment, Virgil then reached in his jacket's inside pocket and took out another envelope and handed it over to Sherman. "These are the negatives. For most clients I keep a set for myself. For my own protection. But not about this. Not about you. No, you have everything. And, Pastor…" He looked once again up into the camera. "I highly suggest that you destroy that security tape."

As Pastor Sherman looked up at the camera himself, eyes wet with sadness, Virgil clicked the television off. "As you can see, since you're now watching the tape yourselves, he did *not* heed my instructions."

Sheffield gave Virgil a glare and said, "Though what it reveals greatly pains me, in the interest of truth, I'm glad he did not. It wasn't proper for you to suggest it Virgil."

Scolded, but his job done, Virgil sat back down and let the meeting continue. Shonda felt underwater. Before that video she had been so quick to speak up, so sure the man had no reason to commit murder. Now, as the board all debated and discussed their next measures, Brice watched as she fell silent now. Her eyes to the ground, but now something made a lot more sense. "At least now I know why he was silent. Who he was protecting." Her mind was racing, anger building, thinking now of nothing but confronting one person.

Her mother.

CHAPTER FIVE

"How could you!?!" Shonda's words echoed off the walls of the giant, empty house, holding nothing back from the woman that gave her life.

Her mother just shook before her, awash in guilt and shame. She simply broke down, dropping to the floor in a ball and sobbing in grief.

Even though she was angry, Shonda couldn't help but instinctively drop beside her and try to comfort her in this moment. Her eyes, however, were suddenly sharp with focus. The bombshell about her mother had distracted her so much that she had almost forgotten about the case. Something about the fury of emotion had cleansed her, given her a sense of clarity. Holding her mother, her focus was distant.

"I'm so sorry," her mother's lip quivered as she looked up into her daughter's eyes, and went into further details of the relationship that she deeply regretted. She explained it was only to fill a void brought on by her constant loneliness of Sherman being so married to the church. Shonda was in investigator mode however, rifling through the case in her mind. The holes. The mysteries. "Why did he write him a letter? If he was going to kill him. Why didn't he destroy that tape?" A husband who was truly guilty of murdering his wife's assumed lover would know that he would be the first one the cops would look at as a suspect. However, only in the movies would this be the perfect murder – a killer seemingly leaving a trail of clues beforehand that would raise reasonable doubt if the case ever made it to trial. The same 'whys' that Shonda had right now would be the same 'whys' any sane jury would ask themselves.

Shonda's mind was still cycling in Brice's passenger seat later. "He would have known Virgil knew. Anyone could have watched those tapes: Donna. Sheffield. You. I've defended dozens of murderers, and they all have one thing in common."

Brice was in awe, watching her sift through the clues. "You think even faster than you text."

She waved him off, mind awhirl. "None of them think they'll get caught. If Sherman did this– there's too many signs; he'd *know* he'd be the prime suspect. None of it makes sense."

Shaking his head, Brice thought back to the world he had seen as a cop. "I don't know, Shonda, people do some crazy things. Crimes of passion, you know?"

She nodded. "I know. I've represented plenty of those too. But you know what people never do in a crime of passion?"

Brice lifted an eyebrow. "What's that?"

"They never write the victim a handwritten letter. There's the morgue. Turn in here."

Brice had seen his share of dead bodies, but most of Shonda's experience had been in pictures. That said, she had seen *a lot* of pictures of corpses in her work; sometimes, she had even blown them up full-size and put them on display in a courtroom just for the effect. The visceral reaction it brought out was often a valuable tool in a case. It made a death not just a topic of debate, but a ghastly look at mortality for the jury. That sickness that you get in the pit of your stomach at the true sight of death was there with Shonda as she and Brice looked upon the body of Marshall Cooper.

The coroner stood by as they considered the body, taking note of severe damage done to the victim's face. "Cause of death is blunt force trauma to the head. We believe no tool was used, however."

Brice winced as he thought. "The killer did this with his own hands?"

The coroner nodded. "Perhaps by slamming his head repeatedly into a wall or table. There are surfaces all over the victim's kitchen, patio, and pool area that support this. I'll be checking the home myself again tomorrow to do some blood splatter tests and check for the DNA of anyone other than Mr. Cooper."

Shonda saw the remnants of the bloody letter next, lying on another cold steel table beside the man's body. She bent over it – definitely easier to examine a piece of paper than a dead body, even blood-soaked as it was. Just as she had been told, there were only a few legible words, all in her stepfather's unmistakably gorgeous, flowing handwriting. Damning words indeed: *I know what you did and this is how I want to forgive you…*

"Were you able to discover any more parts of this? In– um, inside of him? Or is that impossible?"

The coroner shook his head. "Not impossible at all. We checked for force-feeding and found nothing. If the rest of that letter were forced down his throat, we would definitely find at least the remnants of that."

Brice examined the paper with her. "It looks like this piece was torn before it was shoved in his mouth."

Shonda nodded and headed for the door. "Which means the rest of it is still somewhere. I'm betting it's still at the house."

The coroner called after them, "The police have already been searching for it–"

"Well, I hope they're ready for help. Brice, let's go!"

The drive to the scene of the crime was a quiet one at first. While at a stoplight, Brice took a quick moment to send a text, but all the while he could tell that Shonda's mind was churning, but it was different somehow. She seemed to be dwelling more emotionally, less cerebral. No wild texting or calling out leads and ideas. Her eyes were distantly lost in the horizon. He wondered if the sight of the dead man had shaken her. "You alright, over there? Helping, not hindering. I know that was a lot to see."

She laid her head back and sighed to the ceiling of the car. "Just another casualty in the war of love. How can anyone trust another anymore? It always ends up like this."

Brice's eyes popped. "Whoa whoa. Every relationship does *not* end in murder."

She let out a short laugh. "No, I know. Of course not. I'm just saying, in my experience, every marriage ends in some kind of awful life-changing tragedy. Sorry, being raised by my parents didn't exactly teach me that love is something to seek out."

He let that sad idea float in the air for a long moment. Brice had always found her attractive, but the word around the church body was to approach at your own risk. She never slowed down for a relationship, something everyone around her saw as the missing piece to her near-perfect life. He knew that a harried professional lifestyle didn't always leave room for romance. It didn't seem like something she was ready to budge on, but Brice couldn't let it go unchallenged. "Hey, stay open in life, okay?"

She gave a bit of a hiss through her teeth and shook her head. "Are you serious? Do you have any idea how un-open I've had to live my life? I've had to fight so hard for every step up I've ever made. There was no way to do that amongst all the frat boys at my firm without making sure they knew that romance was out of the question. I've never been able to slow down long enough to even consider it.

Brice let that be the end of the conversation. Those words were hard to hear from a woman that he had always found interesting, beautiful. He shook the thoughts out of his head and continued to drive. *Forget it, Brice. She's not interested. In you. Or anybody apparently.*

They arrived at 4201 South Point Circle just as two police officers were driving off, leaving the cold crime scene for the night in search of other active ones. Brice smacked the dash. "Too late. I'm sorry, Shonda, I didn't know they'd leave so early." He looked to her, and saw a mischievous glimmer in her eye.

She raised a brow. "You're kidding, right? We're totally going in."

"Shonda, it's breaking and entering. We can't– oh, man."

She was already out of the car, huddling into the bushes beside the house and heading down hill around the back. This was a *humble* home, Shonda found herself thinking. Well put together, but set apart up in the woods on a steep hill, almost a cliff, so far from the bustle of the city. She could imagine how a man that lived in secret like this might appeal to a woman like her mother, desperate for some true peace and seclusion from the harried world of being the "always-on" wife of a mega-church pastor. "Don't you even think about it, Shonda. No sympathy for her. Yet. Not until we clear that man's name."

Back in the car, Brice's eyes were shut tight. He was torn between bending the law with this woman for a good cause, or waiting until morning. Couldn't it wait until morning? "Brice, you're such a pushover," he grunted to himself as he stepped out of the car, closed the door quietly, and followed Shonda down to the back patio behind the house.

He found her at the glass patio door, her Louboutin held aloft, ready to use it to break the glass of the back door. "What are you doing! Stop that!" He grasped her by the wrist. "Not a chance. If we're doing this, we're doing it in a way that *won't* let the cops know we were here."

She pulled at the door to show him – locked up tight. "And how do you propose we do that Sherlock?"

He gave a wry smile as he started to look around the patio. "It may sound stupid, but in all my years I have never lost faith in two things. God–" he trailed off as he searched the flower pots, a tool box, and finally gave a laugh of success as he opened the grill and looked inside. "–And fake rocks." He lifted a plastic stone and shook it with a jingle. It was one of those tiny novelty key-hiders you can get at any hardware store. With a cocky stride, he unlocked the door. "Always works, but I admit it's not as sexy."

Shonda smiled. *Sexy, huh?* She was eager to get inside and had to give him the win on this one. She also didn't mind the slight flirtation either. Just the touch of her hand on his shoulder as they moved inside sent a spark of electricity through them both. They both couldn't help but enjoy this midnight mischief with an attractive member of the opposite sex, but they both made sure to drop the romance as they stepped inside and got to work.

"The cops would have rolled this place over looking for the rest of that notebook. We're going to need to be on the hunt for every secret hiding place if we're going to find where Cooper kept that letter. Maybe the guy had a hidden safe or a secret compartment somewhere."

Brice nodded and headed further into the house. "I'll take upstairs, you take down."

They split up, leaving the lights off in the house to avoid attracting attention.

Shonda found the office and, by the light of the moon shining through the windows, started to search. She had a private safe in her own home office, activated by the push of a fake piece of wood siding in her bookcase; but it was going to take a while to find out exactly where a total stranger kept his darkest secrets. She traced her fingers along every shelf, feeling under the desk, finding nothing. It was moments like these, when an almost-impossible task seemed desperate, where she *did* find herself yearning for the aid of God. She found herself silently praying in her head for the divine guidance that was needed to lead her. *I don't believe he did it, Lord. He's truly one of yours. Help me. However it is that you want me to save this man, let me do it. For you. And for my soul's peace as well.*

Sometimes, however, God doesn't answer your prayers in a way that's anywhere close to a happy miracle. Sometimes, he answers with what seems like a horrible, screaming *no*.

Shonda heard the unmistakable *click* – the cocking of a pistol.

The presence of a gun filled her with such sudden and total fear that she spun, knowing that the sound must have come from right behind her. The fear made the tiny sound so loud. There was no one there, however. She was still alone in the room, but she could now hear creaking floorboards and careful but heavy steps coming from back in the other room, having entered through the same door as her, no doubt. She huddled, terrified, in the shadows and pieced together a new truth that was so simple and awful that she cursed her naïve mind for not realizing it earlier. *Oh God. Oh, of course. I already know who is in this house with me. I'm a fool. A dead fool. Because Brice is the killer. You silly little schoolgirl. Blinded by his strong arms and simple flirtations. Now you've gotten too close. So he came along to kill you too. See what happens when you let things cloud your mind, ruin your judgment.*

It all made perfect sense. Even as she waited with dread for her executioner to round the corner, her investigatory brain couldn't help but complete the puzzle with her last dying thoughts. Brice was a man whose life had been saved by Pastor Sherman – who considered himself indebted to him, only to see him shamefully cuckolded by a cheating wife and some stranger across town. He must have seen the security tapes, how his pastor was going to take it lying down like a sheep, and it drove him insane. He acted in revenge for the man that he felt brought him to salvation. And any clues found in this house could potentially lead to him being the killer, and he couldn't let that happen. Who knows what he had being doing in the other room, perhaps cleaning up evidence. That's it. Case closed, Shonda.

The shadowy figure slowly appeared in the door frame, just as she feared. However, she couldn't make out the face. Brice? She wasn't sure. What happened next surprised Shonda, even as she did it.

She threw a globe at him.

Even as violent chaos erupted right after, Shonda heard two sides of her brain. One side marveling *Did I just–throw a desk globe at a guy with a gun?* The other side could only answer, *Well, what were we supposed to do? Stand there and die?*

The globe batted off of his forehead, and his arms flailed. He pulled the trigger, and the gun went off. *Bang!*

An antique radio on a shelf right next to Shonda burst and splintered, the bullet embedded in the wall right behind it. Shonda ran through a door into the next room, with him aggressively chasing her with determination. She pushed over chairs behind her. He stumbled over them in the dark, waving his gun arm in the air and trying to get a clear shot at her.

She raced through the hall and kitchen toward moonlight she thought was coming from a door, but it was only a locked window. *Trapped.* Shonda pushed on it desperately, hoping to climb through, but it wouldn't budge until–*bang!* Another gunshot. C*rash!* The window exploded, shattered by a stray bullet. He'd missed, and Shonda found herself scrambling out the newly-opened window frame, dropping to the leaves beneath, and rolling down a wooded hill. She skidded, trying to control her fall down the steep ridge. Shonda then kicked off her heels and dug her bare feet into the dirt. She lifted herself to her feet, running headlong into the trees. Looking quickly behind her, she could see he had made the leap down himself, racing after her, still trying to find a shot with his pistol raised right at her.

Then with another quick look behind her, and directly behind the man chasing her, she saw...Brice! It wasn't him that was after her. If not him, then who? Brice was breaking into a wild sprint from the house in pursuit to save the day. It was one of the greatest things she had ever seen, but the woods grew thicker, darker around her. She angled her run to try and throw the man after her off her tracks. Before she knew it, she was just as disorientated.

Slowing her run, she leapt onto some rocks, trying to keep her feet from crunching in the dry leaves and giving away her position. *You've come a long way from clicking your courthouse heels like a diva just this morning.* Shonda slid down behind the rocks and watched the trees, searching for movement.

She was looking the wrong way.

Click.

Shonda shut her eyes tight as she felt the cold steel barrel of the gun press to her temple. But before he could pull the trigger, Brice leapt from the trees and tackled him. The gun flew into the darkness as they rolled into a brutal wrestle through the brush. Each man traded vicious blows to the ribs. The man grasped Brice by the back of the head and bashed his face into a tree stump. Again. *Again.*

"Stop!" Shonda cried, seeing him bashing Brice the very way she assumed Marshall Cooper must've been killed the night before. Brice shifted his weight and struggled to maintain consciousness as the two men strained every muscle, trying to best each other until–

Whack!

The man went limp in Brice's hands. Brice pushed him off of him and saw Shonda standing above with a large, heavy branch in her arms. It was broken. She had brought it down hard on the man's head. She was gasping, and so was Brice, but she smiled. "Sorry, I know you heroes like to take the bad guys out yourselves."

He smiled wide at this, even as he pressed a hand to his bleeding face. "Does it look like I care which one of us knocked him out? I just consider it you—" and they both finished his sentence together, "–helping. Not hindering."

"Who is he?" Shonda asked, breathless.

Brice took a closer look. "I recognize him. His name's Willie, a two-bit burglar I busted a few times back in the day. He's gotta rap sheet as long as my arm. Must've been casing the place."

"Or returning to the scene of the crime," Shonda guessed.

"Maybe."

Police sirens could be heard in the background. Someone must've heard the gunshots and made the call. Shonda would head back up to meet them, while Brice remained behind – retrieving Willie's gun from the ground and holding him at bay.

Within seconds, Willie began to come to, moaning and trying to nurse the blow to his head by applying pressure with his hand. Standing, he soon turned to Brice and mumbled, "What are you doing? This wasn't the plan."

Wait. What?

"Change of plans Willie. You played your part." With a squeeze of the trigger and a bang, Brice sent Willie flat on his back. With only minutes to spare, Brice quickly removed a knife from his backside. He went over to Willie and pressed the handle in his right hand for fingerprints. He then tossed it on the ground next to his lifeless body.

When the police and paramedics arrived with Shonda leading the way, Brice was on his knees performing chest compressions on Willie. "He came at me with a knife," he explained, while pretending to save the life of a man he already knew was gone.

EMT took over and soon pronounced him dead.

A detective would eventually take their statements of the events that had transpired. Brice would go on to explain that Willie came to and pulled a knife – and after telling him to drop it and he didn't, he was left with no choice but to fire.

Another officer soon brought Shonda and Brice inside the house to show them an amazing discovery. They had uncovered Marshall Cooper's secret stash of papers after all, they were spilling out of the antique radio that had been shattered by the wild gun shot. There, indeed, was the rest of Pastor Sherman's letter. Only a few words needed to be read to exonerate him and understand the full nature of the man and this missive he had written to the man who had been involved with his wife: *I know what you did, and this is how I want to forgive you. First, know that my wife means the world to me, and I love her more than life itself. But I know that in order to truly forgive her, I also must forgive you. But my forgiveness, I'm afraid, must come at a distance, but it also comes with an invitation. I can never come to you personally, for my pain is too great. I'm only flesh and blood. But if you ever wish true forgiveness for your sins, go to the Lord. My church can help, if needed. It wouldn't be easy for me, but I could weather the storm if you were truly seeking redemption. Many sinners like you, and I, have found peace at Mountaintop. Who knows? God works in mysterious ways. So does forgiveness. So does love. You just have to make that first step. Sincerely in Christ, Sherman Richards.*

Wow, it was an actual letter of forgiveness. Shonda couldn't believe the humility and peace showcased by her stepfather in the letter. It was unreal. No way he could have killed him.

Brice let out a deep, emotional exhale. "I'm sure this will play a big part in helping to set him free, along with any other evidence the police may find. And especially if they find out Willie is somehow connected to this. But–"

She finished his sentence for him." But the person that needed to read this, *was me*."

That Sunday, Sherman delivered his sermon to Mountaintop Church, just a week after he'd been arrested for murder – then cleared and freed based on evidence that placed Willie at the scene the night of the murder. It was chalked up as a burglary gone wrong. The sermon on forgiveness with a dash of "Thou shalt not kill." was timely. It was also the first of the pastor's sermons to ever be published by the local, secular press. They spun it as a human interest story. *Innocent man arrested for murder delivers message of mercy.* The church board had, of course, reinstated all faith in the pastor since he was cleared.

After the service, Pastor Sherman took Shonda aside. "I'm sorry I didn't mention you in the sermon. I thought about it, but it felt–"

She waved this off. "No, no. Are you kidding? Your message was perfect. The world is better for you having said it."

His eyes drank her in with deep pride and gratitude. "Thank you, Shonda."

With an eye roll, she tried to back him down. "Pastor Sher– Dad, you've thanked me constantly ever since–"

He wouldn't be silenced. "Since you saved my life? Days ago? Don't you think a guy might wanna thank you a few too many times for that?"

He meant more than just keeping him out of jail, however. Their eyes locked, a deep trust there. "Thank you for believing in me. I know sometimes, while it was all going on, that it must have been difficult – some doubt.

She took this truth in, and allowed herself to give a soft nod. He assured her that it was okay.

As they regarded each other with even greater respect, both of them saw her mother exit the church. She saw them and carefully approached. Grace had watched the service from the back. There were many in the church that would have a great deal of trouble forgiving her. She knew it, and so did her husband and daughter.

Shonda whispered to him, "Is she going to be alright, Dad? Are the two of you–"

He exhaled. "It's going to be a long road. But Shonda? I think the three of us have a lot of road left. Lord willing."

As Grace reached their side, her face was downcast. She was wracked with guilt and terrified of how her family would act towards her. Pastor Sherman did all he could, which was raise a hand and gingerly press it to her arm. It was a slight touch, but from a man that had truly and deeply been hurt.

Shonda, however, gave her a hug and took her hand. "Come on, Mom. Let's head home." Grace's eyes were wet with emotion; it meant a lot for Shonda to reach out in that way. Pastor Sherman watched as they moved on. Shonda was learning much about forgiveness indeed.

As her mom headed in the direction of the car, Shonda saw Brice keeping watch in the parking lot. He waved vehicles along and assisted the elderly parishioners into the shuttle to the nearby nursing home. When he was free, he moved to Shonda, and the two regarded each other with a deep sense of connection. Both of them didn't know how to begin, but Shonda tried to ease the moment with humor. "I've kind of had a hell of a week. You?"

He laughed at this and looked to his shoes. They both realized they were acting like nervous schoolkids. Yet, he offered her a way out.

"Listen, um– we went through a lot together and– I'm not sure that's the right way for two people to– I'm just saying I understand. If you– we don't have to–"

"Hey, you wanna go out sometime? Maybe catch a movie? Or another killer?"

This made them both double over in laughter. She rested a hand on his shoulder, easy and comfortable. Across the church campus, Pastor Sherman and several members of the church watched this with a smile. Brice gave a wry smile. "Yes. Yeah. I would love that. You promise you don't think it's weird though, right? How this– us– is all getting started?"

Shonda bit her lip playfully. She had to admit, it wasn't at all how she'd imagined starting a relationship. When she took his hand, however, it was with a tender longing that she suspected would never go away. "Something he said in that letter really awoke something inside me. About the *Lord working in mysterious ways.*"

Brice nodded. Shonda smiled as she dreamt of the possibilities. "So – you wanna work in mysterious ways a little?"

They both smiled and talked for a few minutes more, and soon parted with plans to see each other later. Brice made his way over to Reverend Sherman who regarded him with a smile and a firm handshake of appreciation.

"She's going to make some man a wonderful wife," he said to Brice.

"I have no doubt," Brice replied.

The two men stood quietly only for a few seconds, Sherman taking a much needed deep breath, thankful for his freedom among other things. His gaze was on his wife as she and Shonda prepared to leave. He gave a small wave to Grace who had briefly looked his way. He himself couldn't take his eyes off of her, his smile gradually turning into a frown.

Then, Sherman, his tone and demeanor suddenly changing from the man everyone knew and loved, as if someone else had embodied him both mentally and spiritually, glanced towards Brice and said, "Make it look like an accident."

Enjoyed this story?
If so, please leave a kind review on Amazon.
Your support is appreciated, never forgotten.

Join my Mailing List
Friend me on Facebook
and stay informed of books to come or
visit me at www.edwarddeanarnold.com.

FOUL
(COMING SOON)

Keith woke up unable to move. His muscles immediately burst back into struggle mode, his brain still believing he was in the midst of a fight... but he wasn't.

He was restrained to a hospital bed. At the first sign of his consciousness, half a dozen figures in the room rushed to his side to try and steady him quickly. "Mr. Jacobs, please. You're safe. Stop struggling." "He'll tear his bandages." Hands were all over him, bright lights in his face he didn't recognize. He wasn't just restrained, there were pins sticking out of him! Wrappings all over him – including half of his face. His vision was marred by one eye being covered. What was happening?

"Keith, baby, stop this. It's me."

It was this final voice that brought him back – Gabriella – she rushed to his side and stroked the side of his face that wasn't bandaged. It made his struggling start to subside and he slowly steadied himself as best he could. His eyes were tearing. Hers were too. There was a relief far in the back of his mind that he was alive at all, but he could tell from the look in her eyes that he was about to hear awful news about his body. There were such extensive bindings and work that had obviously already been done. Life was about to never be the same.

"Mr. Jacobs, I want to stress how lucky you are to still be alive."

It sounded to Keith like he had been listening to his doctor from the bottom of a deep pool. Though, the information was vital, he was hardly listening – picking up the basics – he had been beaten within an inch of his life. He had broken bones all over, cracked ribs, broken leg, his face was all busted up…

… but his shooting hand. That was the part of him that made him shudder to look at – even think about. His right hand had been absolutely shattered. He couldn't move it, drugs meant he couldn't even feel it, which he was told was a mercy.

"Believe me, Mr. Jacobs, if it weren't for the meds, your entire body… the pain would probably send you back into unconsciousness. You certainly wouldn't be able to concentrate on this conversation with me."

He wasn't concentrating, Doctor. Keith's brain was whirling in a downward spiral into what those vicious thugs had done to him, all he had lost. Was this possible? When was he going to be able to get back on the court? To prove to the world that he was still number one? Though it filled him with horror, he looked back at his motionless hand – there were pins sticking out of it from every angle! How long before he could sink another three with that!

The doctor continued, "Truly, sir, I need you to be prepared for the fact that working your way back to health is now about to become your full time and only job."

Keith shook his head as best he could (which was not much), "When will I play again? Championships are just weeks away."

The doctor looked to the floor – he hated this part of his job. Gabriella was there by his side, gripping his shoulder – one of the few parts of his body showing enough bare, healthy flesh for her to comfort him by. Keith was alive, but the doctor delivered a cold and clinical diagnosis that was just as terrifying as death.

"Mr. Jacobs, it is a very real possibility that you will never be able to play basketball again."

Gabriella did her best. She was a woman used to VIP sections and bottle service at the hottest clubs in the world every night. Here she was instead, expected to spend time in a silent, sad hospital room, next to a guy who looked more like puzzle pieces shaken out of a box than a whole man. Keith was losing track of time, sometimes on purpose – he just wanted to lose himself.

Instead, he seemed to have a unending number of people that needed to speak to him. He knew his agent would do his best to keep the NBA and the press at bay – who knew how much money and how many trophies were in the wind because of Keith's state. Neither Gabriella or his management team could do anything to keep the police out, however. There were, after all, five brutal bastards out there on the loose - the men that had done this to him. Keith didn't mind the cops' presence because the thirst for revenge that seethed within knew they were his best bet at anything that looked like vengeance.

Thank you.

CPSIA information can be obtained
at www.ICGtesting.com
Printed in the USA
BVHW031519260620
582395BV00003B/142